C000050523

The Dragon of Cyprus

By Tom Noble

Illustrated by Luke Morrisby

All correspondence to the author:
tom.noble@ncc.qld.edu.au

First Printed 2020

ISBN: 978-0-6489739-2-8

Donatello was an athletic young man, full of zest for life. Sadly, a sickness had swept through his village in Italy. Many people had died, including his family. Alone, and looking for adventures, he boarded a boat and sailed south to the Isle of Cyprus to become a knight.

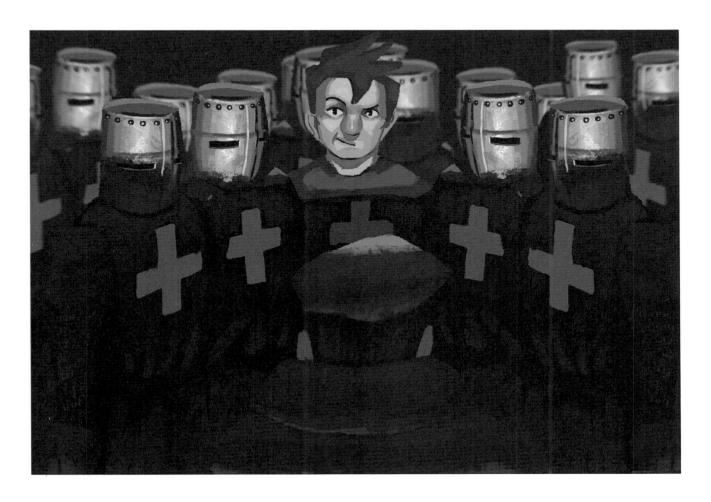

By noble birthright and oaths of service to God, Donatello became a knight of the Order of Saint John. He proudly received his armour and black tunic with a white cross and was welcomed by the Mayor of Cyprus with the other recruits. During the ceremony they were given the warning that knights were forbidden to visit the southern tip of the island, for a dragon had made a nest in the limestone cliffs. From all accounts the creature was extremely fierce. Not only had it devoured sheep, but on three occasions knights had also disappeared.

Immediately curious, Donatello and his new friends went to investigate. They had heard of dragons but had never seen one. From a safe distance the young recruits observed the creature lying in the full sun on the seashore. It was the size of a lion with powerful legs and a long scaly neck and tail. It had dual colours of dolphin grey and honey and had small transparent wings. Collecting the rays of the winter sun, the metallic colours shimmered on its wet skin.

Disobedient Donatello thought this was a chance to make a name for himself. He convinced a village boy who owned a hunting dog to accompany him. They set off, Donatello leading the way, equipped with lance, sword and shield.

They found the dragon's cave and cautiously entered. For a moment all was quiet, then suddenly the monster sprang out of the darkness with a frenzied warning display of snarling teeth, hissing breath and slashing claws. Instinctively, the hunting dog distracted the dragon by barking and charging back and forth. Seizing his opportunity, Donatello aimed his sharp lance at the dragon's throat and skilfully thrust it forward.

Although the dragon was hurt it instantly spun around to strike down the knight with its spiky tail. Terrified, the dog and the boy fled in fear. The knight and the dragon lay wounded and exhausted on the floor of the cave. For the first time, Donatello could clearly see the eyes of the dragon and recognised a fellow creature. In that moment, he saw a rare and magnificent creation. It dawned on him that it may be the last dragon left alive. He would fight it no longer.

Somehow the Mayor discovered Donatello's defiance and had him arrested and imprisoned in the castle dungeon. During his time in prison, he reflected on his encounter and regretted his violent intentions. However, fame and glory remained his goals. Eventually, the old Mayor passed away and Donatello was released. As he walked the streets, a free knight again, he heard that a new Mayor was to be elected. It was now time to put his plan into action. He visited the dragon, alone this time, with a sack of fish and chickens. It recognised him instantly and became agitated but was soon won over by his kind manner and generous offerings of food.

After a month of visits, the two were fully reconciled and had developed a bond of trust. The dragon allowed Donatello to touch his head and even ride on his back! The young knight was astounded at the agility and acceleration.

On the day that the nominations for Mayor closed and the election was being held, Donatello and the dragon achieved the unthinkable. To shrieks of villagers and the awe of the knights, Donatello rode through the village up to the castle on the back of the proud dragon and nominated himself for the vacant position. The vote was unanimous.

Donatello, with the mighty dragon at his side, was elected to be the new ruler of Cyprus.

Author's Inspiration

The Dragon Slayer who was elected Grand Master of the Order

There was a young man named **Dieudonné de Gozon** who joined the Order of Knights of the Hospital of Saint John of Jerusalem, commonly known as the Knights Hospitaller of Malta.

Apparently after slaying a 'dragon' and hanging its head on the town gate, Gozon successfully campaigned to become the Grand Master of the Order from 1346 to 1353.

Reference: https://www.britishmuseum.org/collection/term/BIOG106607

This story was apparently well known in medieval times and is recorded in several sources including 'The History of the Knights of Malta'.

Reference: https://www.um.edu.mt/library/oar/bitstream/123456789/10785/1/The%20hospitallers%27%20early%20written%20records.pdf

Reference: https://www.cambridge.org/core/books/history-of-the-knights-of-malta/86B7F02085870D22EBFBF56D4CC6A2CF

Image 1: *Accessed on 20/11/2020 from https://en.wikipedia.org/wiki/Dieudonné_de_Gozon*

In latin, his gravestone reads 'Ci git le vainqueur du draco' or in English...

'Here lies the vanquisher of the dragon'.

Image 2: *Tombstone of Dieudonné de Gozon. Musée de Cluny.*
https://en.wikipedia.org/wiki/Dieudonn%C3%A9_de_Gozon#/media/File:DieudonneDeGozonTombstone.jpg

Lightning Source UK Ltd.
Milton Keynes UK
UKRC012208151220
375316UK00002B/8